Karen's School

**Look for these
and other books about Karen
in the
Baby-sitters Little Sister series:**

Little Sister

Karen's School
Ann M. Martin

Illustrations by Susan Tang

A
LITTLE APPLE
PAPERBACK

SCHOLASTIC INC.
New York Toronto London Auckland Sydney

No part of this publication may be reproduced in whole or in part, or stored in a retrieval system, or transmitted in any form or by any means, electronic, mechanical, photocopying, recording, or otherwise, without written permission of the publisher. For information regarding permission, write to Scholastic Inc., 730 Broadway, New York, NY 10003.

ISBN 0-590-47041-8

12 11 10 9 8 7 6 5 4 3   6 7 8/9

Printed in the U.S.A.   40

First Scholastic printing, September 1993

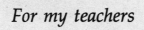
For my teachers

Autumn

"What makes people different?" asked my teacher Ms. Colman.

"We look different," said Natalie Springer.

"Yes," agreed Ms. Colman. "What else?"

"We like different things," said Hank Reubens.

"Very good," said Ms. Colman. "Our tastes make us different. Our likes and dislikes. What else?"

I did not hear the answer to Ms. Colman's question. I began thinking about my tastes, about the things I like and the things I do not like. Some of my most favorite things are the seasons. Winter, spring, summer, fall. I like every one of them, for different reasons. I like winter because I like snow. I like spring because I like flowers and baby animals. I like summer because I like vacations. And I like fall because I like going back to school and I like holidays.

When September comes I know that Halloween is just around the corner. After Halloween comes Thanksgiving. And then comes Christmas and then New Year's Eve and then Valentine's Day and then Easter. My friend Nancy Dawes celebrates some different holidays. In the fall she celebrates Rosh Hashanah (that's the Jewish New Year), and then Yom Kippur and then Hanukkah and then Passover. . . .

"Karen? Are you paying attention?" Ms. Colman asked me.

"Yes," I said, even though I wasn't.

Usually, I try to pay attention, since I like school so much. I am Karen Brewer. I am

2

in second grade, and Ms. Colman is a gigundoly excellent teacher. I love her. I plan to work very hard. I want Ms. Colman to think I am a gigundoly excellent student. But it was a little hard to pay attention on a warm September day when the windows in our classroom were open. I could look into the courtyard outside. I could see the leaves beginning to turn red and yellow. And I could see a garden. The garden made me think of Daddy's vegetable garden, and that made me think of my pumpkin patch, and the pumpkin patch made me think of pumpkins, and pumpkins made me think of Halloween. . . .

"Pssst. Karen!" Ricky Torres was nudging me. Ricky sits next to me. We sit in the front row. That is because we wear glasses. Ms. Colman makes glasses-wearers sit near the blackboard. Natalie Springer wears glasses, too. She sits on the other side of me.

"What?" I whispered to Ricky.

"Pay attention!" he hissed. (Ricky is my

3

pretend husband. We got married on the playground one day. That is why he cares about me so much.)

I sat up straighter. I looked around my classroom. I looked at Ms. Colman standing by the board. I looked at Bobby Gianelli (the bully) and Hank Reubens, who are Ricky's friends. I looked at Terri and Tammy (the twins) and Addie (who uses a wheelchair) and Pamela (my enemy) and Jannie and Leslie (Pamela's friends). Then I snuck a peek at the back row. There were my two very best friends, Nancy Dawes and Hannie Papadakis. I could sit with them, if I did not wear glasses.

"What else makes us different from each other?" asked Ms. Colman.

I had an answer. (I remembered to raise my hand.) "Our families," I said. "We come from different kinds of families. And families that are different sizes."

I should know. *Nobody* in Ms. Colman's room has a family like mine. In fact, I even have two families.

Karen Has Two Families

Yup. I really do. I have two families. One is small and one is big. I did not always have two families, though. A long time ago, when I was a little kid, I had just one family. Daddy, Mommy, Andrew, and me. (Andrew is my little brother. He is four now, going on five. And I am seven.) My family lived in a gigundo house. It was the house Daddy had grown up in. I thought we were very happy. But then Mommy and Daddy began fighting. They fought a lot. They were not happy at all. Finally they told Andrew and me that they were going to get a divorce. They loved us very much, but they had stopped loving each other.

After the divorce, Mommy and Andrew and I moved into a little house. Daddy stayed in his big house. (Both of the houses are here in Stoneybrook, Connecticut.) Then guess what. Mommy and Daddy got married again. Mommy married Seth. He is my stepfather. Daddy married Elizabeth. She is my stepmother. And that is how Andrew and I got two families.

This is my little-house family: Mommy, Seth, Andrew, me, Rocky, Midgie, and Emily Junior. Rocky and Midgie are Seth's cat and dog. Emily Junior is my rat. I live with my little-house family most of the time.

This is my big-house family: Daddy, Elizabeth, Kristy, Charlie, Sam, David Michael, Emily Michelle, Nannie, Andrew, me, Shannon, Boo-Boo, Goldfishie, and Crystal Light the Second. Kristy, Charlie, Sam, and David Michael are Elizabeth's kids, so they are my stepsister and stepbrothers. I just love Kristy. She is thirteen and she baby-sits. She is the best, best big sister. Charlie and Sam are old. They go to high school. Sam teases, but he is really okay. And Charlie is nice (usually). Sometimes he takes me for a ride in his car, the Junk Bucket. David Michael is okay, too. He is just my age. But he does not go to my school. He goes to Stoneybrook Elementary. I go to Stoneybrook Academy. Guess who Emily Michelle is. She is my adopted sister. Daddy and Elizabeth adopted her from the country of Vietnam. That is very far away. Emily is two and a half. I named my rat after her. Nannie is Elizabeth's mother. That makes her my stepgrandmother. She helps take care of us kids. Shannon, Boo-Boo, Gold-fishie, and Crystal Light are our pets. Shannon is a big floppy puppy. Boo-Boo is a cross old cat. Maybe you can guess what the other two are. (Andrew named Gold-fishie.) I live with my big-house family every other weekend and on some holidays and vacations.

Andrew may not be very good at naming things, but I am. I made up special nicknames for my brother and me. I call us Andrew Two-Two and Karen Two-Two. (I thought of the names after Ms. Colman read aloud a book called *Jacob Two-Two Meets the Hooded Fang*.) Andrew and I are two-twos because we have two of so many things. We have two houses and two families, two mommies and two daddies, two cats and two dogs. Also, I have two bicycles, one at each house. And Andrew has two tricycles. We have clothes and books and toys at each house. (That way we do not have to pack much when we go back and forth.) I have two pieces of Tickly, my special blanket. I have two stuffed cats, Moosie and Goosie, that look just the same. Moosie stays at the big house and Goosie stays at the little house. And of course, I have my two best friends. Nancy lives next door to Mommy. Hannie lives across the street from Daddy and one house down. I even have two pairs of glasses. The blue pair is for reading. The pink pair is for the rest of the time. (Well, I do not have to wear them in bed or in the bathtub, of course.)

So those are my two families. I bet nobody else in Ms. Colman's class has two families, at least not just like mine.

Real School

"Rain, rain, go away. Come again another day. I want to go out and play," sang Andrew. My brother was standing at the kitchen window. He was watching the rain and singing sadly.

"Andrew, rain is good," I told him importantly.

"Not when you want sunshine," he replied.

It was a Saturday morning at the big house. And rain was pouring down. The trees bent back and forth in the wind. The leaves were tossed to the ground. I liked our rainstorm. But Andrew did not. He was bored. That was because he did not have any homework.

Almost everyone else in the big house had homework. Kristy and Sam and Charlie were working in their rooms. Daddy and Elizabeth were working on papers from their briefcases. Emily and Nannie did not have homework, but they were busy cutting shapes out of colored paper. David Michael and I were sitting at the kitchen table. David Michael was filling in the blank spaces on a page from his math workbook. I was writing sentences using words from my new spelling list.

Only Andrew was not busy.

"Karen," said Andrew, "what are you doing?"

"Homework," I replied. "I already told you that."

"What are you doing, David Michael?" he asked.

"The same thing."

"The same homework as Karen?"

David Michael sighed. "No. I am doing math homework. Karen is doing spelling homework." He paused. "And we are very busy."

Andrew edged closer to the table. "What do you do in *real* school, Karen?" he wanted to know. "In big kids' school?"

Here is the thing about Andrew. He goes to school, but he is only old enough for preschool, even though he can already read. This year his teacher is named Miss Jewel. Andrew loves Miss Jewel. He likes school, too. But in his school he mostly paints and listens to stories and plays with trucks and wishes he were five already.

I showed Andrew my homework paper. "This is one thing I do in school," I told him.

Andrew looked at the paper. " 'A friend is someone you can play with,' " he read slowly.

"See? 'Friend' is one of my spelling words," I said. "Ms. Colman told us to

13

make sentences using the words."

Andrew nodded. "So that is what you do in real school. You write. I wish I could write."

I thought about that. Maybe I could teach Andrew to write. After all, I was the one who had taught him to read.

"Andrew, do you want to do big kids' work?" I asked.

"Yes," replied Andrew.

"Well, us big kids learn to write. We also learn about numbers and science and animals and people from other countries."

"And weather," added David Michael.

"You do?" said Andrew.

"Yes," said David Michael and I.

"Would you really like to learn what the big kids learn?" I asked Andrew. (He nodded.) "Okay. I have an idea. But I cannot do anything about it until I finish my homework."

"Then I will be very quiet," said Andrew. He pulled out a kitchen chair. He sat on it.

He folded his hands in his lap.

David Michael and I went back to work. I had a little trouble concentrating on my sentences. I was thinking about my big idea.

Karen's School

"There," I said. "All finished." I read my last sentence over again and made sure I had spelled every word right.

Andrew jumped up. "What is your idea?" he asked me.

"I am going to make a real school for you," I told him. "It will be a place where you can learn what the big kids learn, especially how to write. That is very important."

"How are you going to make a real school for me?" asked Andrew.

"Don't worry. I have already figured it out. First I just need a little peace and privacy. In the playroom. I will call you when I am ready."

I put away my homework. I ran upstairs to the playroom. For a moment I just stood in the doorway and looked around. Then I got to work.

I searched through the toys until I found a chalkboard. I set the chalkboard on an easel. Then I found an eraser and some chalk. I put a little chair at our coloring table. I stood the easel in front of the table. I made a teacher's desk by setting a grown-up-size chair in front of a writing table.

After that I found paper and markers and scissors. I sat at my big desk. I worked busily for a long time. When I finished, I called to Andrew.

He came running. "Is my school ready?" he asked.

"Yes," I replied. "Now, Andrew, this is your first day at your new school. I am your new teacher, and we have never met before."

"We haven't?"

"No," I said. "Now knock at the door."

Andrew knocked on the doorway to the playroom. "Hello?" he called.

"Hello," I replied. "Welcome to school. I am Miss Karen. Who are you?"

"I am Andrew Edward Brewer."

"Won't you come in?" I said. "Now let me see. First I will find your name tag." Andrew's name tag was on my desk. I stuck it to his shirt with a piece of tape. "Now I will not forget who you are," I told him. "Okay, Andrew. This is your desk. Please sit down."

Andrew slid into the seat at the crayon table. "Teach me to write," he said.

"I will. In just a minute. First I have to tell you about school rules. We have lots of rules in real school. If you want to say something, raise your hand. And wait to be called on. No shouting out. Let me see. No chewing gum. No bare feet. No eating unless it is snacktime. Most important, if you do not understand something, be sure to ask questions."

Andrew raised his hand. "When am I going to learn to write?" he wanted to know.

"Now," I replied. I placed a sheet of paper in front of Andrew. On the paper I had written the alphabet in big letters and small letters. I handed Andrew a pencil. "Okay. Trace over these letters," I said.

Andrew began to trace the letters slowly. He stuck his tongue out of the corner of his mouth. He erased a lot. After a few minutes he said, "You — "

"Raise your hand and wait to be called on," I reminded him.

Andrew raised his hand and started over. "You know what?" he said. "This is fun, but a real school would have more kids."

More kids? Hmm. That was a good idea.

"Andrew, stay right here and keep tracing," I told him. "I will come back in a little while." I raced to the phone. I called Hannie.

"Hannie!" I exclaimed. "Great idea! We can start a school for little kids. I will be the teacher and you can be my helper. Andrew is our first student, and we can find some others. Like Emily Michelle."

"And Sari," said Hannie. (Sari is Hannie's little sister.) "Ooh, that *is* a good idea, Karen. You know who else we could ask? Callie and Keith." (Callie and Keith live down the street. They are four, like Andrew. And they are twins.)

"And we can have school on big-house weekends," I added. "Oh, Hannie, come over right now, okay? We have lots of work to do."

Mr. Howard

Hannie and I could not just start a real school like that — snap! We had to plan for it. We had to find students and set up the classroom and decide how we would teach our students. We were going to be very busy for the next couple of weeks.

On Monday, Ms. Colman gave me something to think about besides our school. First thing in the morning, she made one of her Surprising Announcements. She started off by saying, "Girls and boys, do you know how a person becomes a teacher?" She looked at us with raised eyebrows.

"Does she go to school?" asked Pamela.

"Yes," replied Ms. Colman. "First a teacher is a student, just like you are. And she or he goes to school to learn how to be a teacher. Then she practices teaching for a while. She practices in a classroom with someone who is already a teacher, and can help her and show her what to do. She is called a student teacher then."

"Were you a student teacher once?" I asked.

"Yes, I was," said Ms. Colman. "And now it is my turn to help a new student teacher. His name is Mr. Howard, and he is going to practice teaching right here in our classroom. You will meet him later today. He is going to come in to meet you and to watch me teach. He will come in every day for the next six weeks. At first he will teach you for just half an hour or so. Then he will take over the class a little bit more and a little bit more. For the last two weeks of his stay, he will be your only teacher."

"Ms. Colman, where will you be?" I asked. I did not want some new student teacher. I wanted Ms. Colman.

"Oh, I will be here," she replied. "Right here in school. Mostly I will be in the room so I can watch Mr. Howard. But sometimes I will leave the classroom and let him be in charge." Ms. Colman cleared her throat. "Boys and girls," she added, "when Mr. Howard is teaching, I want you to pretend I am not even nearby. And I want you to be polite and well-behaved. I want you to treat Mr. Howard the way you would treat me."

We met Mr. Howard that afternoon. He stood next to Ms. Colman while she introduced him. Mr. Howard smiled at us. One front tooth was crooked. His tie had big blops of color all over it. And his hair was slicked back with tonic. I could smell that tonic from my seat. Right away, I knew I was not going to like Mr. Howard.

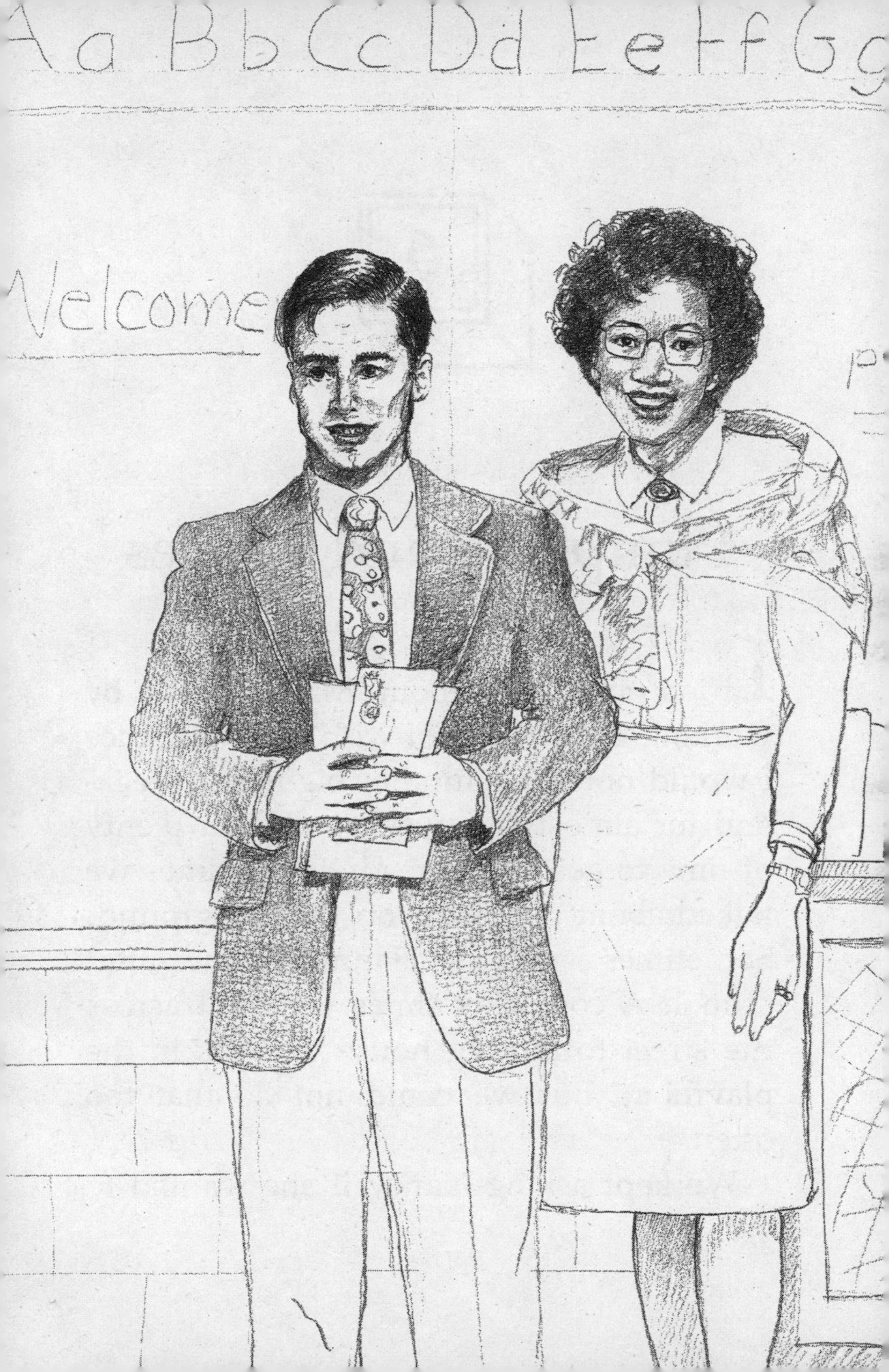
Aa Bb Cc Dd Ee Ff Gg
Welcome

Pumpkins and Leaves

I tried to forget about Mr. Howard by working on my school with Hannie. Since I would not have another big-house weekend for almost two weeks, we had plenty of time to get things ready. Sometimes we talked about our plans on the playground. Sometimes I went to Hannie's house after school. A couple of times we went across the street to the big house to work in the playroom. But we could not do that too often.

We kept asking Nancy if she wanted to

help us with our school, but Nancy said no. She was not being mean. She just seemed busy. Or something. She looked as if she were daydreaming all the time.

"Nancy," I said, "are you positive you do not want to help us with our school? Hannie and I are having fun. And we might need another teacher."

Do you know what Nancy replied? She said, "What? Karen, did you ask me something? Sorry. I was not listening." Then she went back to her daydreaming. A funny little smile was on her face.

So Hannie and I worked by ourselves.

"Ms. Colman has lesson plans," I said to Hannie on the playground one day. "We should have lesson plans, too."

"What are lesson plans?" Hannie asked.

"They are lists of what everybody is supposed to learn. We will make them for our students.. Okay. First we should write down the names of our students."

Hannie pulled a notepad out of her pocket. She wrote: *Sari, Andrew, Emily,*

Keith, Callie. Then she said, "Now what?"

"Well, they should all learn to read and write," I said. "Except Andrew. He only needs to learn how to write. I already took care of the reading."

"They should *all* learn to read and write?!" exclaimed Hannie.

"Yes. Reading and writing are gigundoly important."

"I know. But Sari and Emily are only two and a half. They hardly even *talk.* How are they supposed to read and write?"

"Don't worry. We will teach them," I said.

"But — "

"Hannie, please. I know what I am doing. I am the teacher and you are my helper. I am in charge of Miss Karen's School."

"Okay-ay," sang Hannie.

One afternoon Hannie and I sat in her bedroom. We made teaching materials for our students. We made alphabet tracing sheets like the one I had made for Andrew.

28

We made some flash cards with words and pictures like this:

PIG

We made worksheets for learning sounds and letters. They were just like the worksheets we used to have in kindergarten. Hannie's father made copies of the pages for us at his office.

Another day, we went to the big house. We ran straight to the playroom. I pointed to the writing table. "There is my desk, the teacher's desk," I told Hannie. "But we need more work spaces for our students."

Hannie and I decided that Andrew and Callie and Keith would sit at the little crayon table. Emily and Sari could do their work on the floor. (They like to sit on the floor.) Then we found old towels for resting mats. After that we collected picture books and put them on a bookshelf.

"Now we have a library corner," I said.

"Nice," said Hannie. "But this classroom needs something else. It needs . . . decorations. Like the ones in Ms. Colman's room."

"You're right!" I exclaimed.

We went back to Hannie's house. We got out the scissors and paper again. We cut out pumpkins and leaves and ghosts and apples. Our classroom was almost ready for its students.

Charlie and the Chocolate Factory

Guess what. For half an hour every day, Mr. Howard was our teacher. Ms. Colman sat in the back of our classroom. She did not say a word. She just watched Mr. Howard learn how to be a teacher.

I thought Mr. Howard had a long way to go.

Mr. Howard's neckties were horrible. (I love Ms. Colman's clothes.) Mr. Howard never wore nice striped ties like Daddy and Seth and my brothers wear. He wore flowered ones or ones with pictures on them, or ones that were orange and pink. And he always gooped up his hair with that smelly stuff. Worst of all, Mr. Howard was not as patient as Ms. Colman. Sometimes he raised his voice. He was *very* strict about our classroom rules. He did not smile as much as Ms. Colman. But he did like to tell jokes. I thought they were stupid jokes. Everyone else thought they were funny. (Nancy thought they were hysterical.)

On the very first day that Ms. Colman let Mr. Howard teach for a while, this is what Mr. Howard said to us: "Class, while I am here, I am going to teach a unit about the book *Charlie and the Chocolate Factory*, by Roald Dahl. So the first thing I am going to do is read the book to you."

I raised my hand. "Mr. Howard, excuse me. I have already read that story," I said. "More than once." (You would think Mr. Howard would want to teach us something new.)

"That's okay," replied Mr. Howard. "We

Spelling

pg. 23

are going to be doing lots of things besides reading the story."

"Okay," I said. I would have to wait and see.

So Mr. Howard had been reading *Charlie and the Chocolate Factory* a little bit each day. I did not think he was very good at reading aloud. He was certainly not as good as Ms. Colman. Ms. Colman tells us to read with expression. And she reads with lots of expression herself. But not Mr. Howard. Plus, he was not very good at switching voices.

On the day he read the end of the book to us, I felt wiggly. I could not sit still in my seat. But everyone else was sitting still just fine. My classmates liked Mr. Howard. I did not understand. How could they look so interested?

When school was over that day I ran back to Hannie and Nancy. Nancy was smiling. She looked faraway. And do you know what she said? She said, "I have a secret. I love Mr. Howard."

The Love Poem

Well, for heaven's sake. Nancy *loved* Mr. Howard. I wondered if she was *in* love with him. That would be interesting.

If Nancy was in love with Mr. Howard it would explain a lot of things. Mostly, it would explain why she did not want to work on Miss Karen's School with Hannie and me. For almost two weeks now Hannie and I had been busy. We had been planning what we would teach our students. We had been setting up our classroom. And we had been making those decorations. Usually, the Three Musketeers work on projects together. But Nancy was not working on Miss Karen's School. Now I thought I knew why.

I thought I knew a few other things, too. I thought I knew what Nancy was daydreaming about all the time. (Mr. Howard.) I thought I knew why she had been getting so dressed up for school. Do you know what she had been wearing? Party dresses and ribbons in her hair and her very best shoes. Once, her mother even let her curl her hair.

Another thing. Nancy kept bringing little gifts to school. And she left them on the teacher's desk — but only when Mr. Howard was sitting at it. One day she brought him a tiny, intsy pumpkin. Another day she brought him a little bouquet of fall flowers. (They have a L-O-O-O-O-N-G name.) And yesterday she brought him two pieces of candy.

I hoped she was not hurting Ms. Colman's feelings.

On Friday, Hannie and Nancy and I were standing in the back of our classroom. We were waiting for Ms. Colman to come in.

"Well," I said, "tomorrow Miss Karen's School will open."

"I cannot wait," replied Hannie.

"I hope our students *like* our school."

"Oh, they will love it," said Hannie. "Especially the decorations."

"Are you sure you do not want to help us, Nancy?" I asked.

Nancy did not answer. I do not think she had heard me. She was all dressed up again, and she was searching through her purse. "Karen? Hannie?" she said. "I have something to show you. I — I wrote a poem. I want to know if you think it is good. You have to tell me the truth."

"Okay," said Hannie and I. (We like poetry.)

Nancy pulled a piece of paper out of her

purse. She unfolded it. She held it out to us. "Go ahead. Read it," she said.

Hannie and I bent over. This is what we read:

Ode to Mr. Howard

Oh, dear Mr. Howard
You are the best.
You are much better
Than all of the rest.
You are better than spring
You are better than fall.
You are better than
   All of them
    All of them,
     All.

Luckily, Nancy had not written her name on the paper.

"What do you think?" Nancy asked. She looked at Hannie and me hopefully.

I glanced at Hannie. "Um, it is beautiful," I said.

38

"Oh, thank you!" cried Nancy. Then she leaned forward and whispered, "Would one of you leave it on Mr. Howard's desk for me? Please? I cannot do it. I am too nervous."

Well, I was certainly not going to give a love poem to smelly Mr. Howard, but I did not want to say so to Nancy, since she was in love with him. Luckily, Hannie said she would do it. (There are some things you just do not understand about your best friends.)

I was glad Miss Karen's School could take my mind off Mr. Howard.

The First Day of School

"First day of school! First day of school!" I called. I ran through the big house ringing a bell. *Ding, ding, ding.*

It was Saturday. And it was almost time for Miss Karen's School to begin.

"Come along, Andrew. Come along, Emily," I said.

"Skoo?" said Emily.

"That's right," I replied. "School. You are going to learn to read, just like Andrew. And you are both going to learn to write."

"I can write my name," said Andrew.

"Well, soon you will be able to write much more than that."

I opened the door to the playroom. I let Andrew and Emily inside. Then I heard the doorbell ring downstairs.

"Oh, good," I said. "I think my other students are here."

Sure enough, a few moments later, Hannie came into the playroom with Sari. "I brought Callie and Keith, too," she said.

Callie and Keith peeped into the room. They looked a little shy.

"Come on inside," I told them.

"Hi, Keith! Hi, Callie!" called Andrew. "Hey, did you see our fish? Here are Goldfishie and Crystal Light. Gold — "

"Andrew," I interrupted him. "This is school. We are here to work. Now, Callie, you and Keith and Andrew sit at this table. You each have your own chair and your own place. Emily and Sari will sit at their work space on the floor. Hannie, you watch them, okay?"

My students slid quietly into their places.

"All right, now. The first thing we do at *real* school," I said, "is take roll. When I call your name, raise your hand and say, 'Here!' "

All of my students were present. I checked off their names on a list.

"Now for school rules," I went on.

"Hey, Keith," whispered Andrew. "Do you want — "

"Ahem!" I said loudly. "The first school rule is no talking while I am talking. Also, you have to raise your hand if you want to say anything. Then you have to wait for me to call on you. . . . Hannie, what are Emily and Sari doing?"

"They're, um, playing," answered Hannie.

"No playing!" I cried. "This is real school!"

"But Karen, they cannot just sit here," said Hannie. "They do not sit still for very long. Especially without something to do."

I sighed. Then I checked my watch. "Well, it is time to start working anyway.

We have a schedule. We need to stick to it. Okay, you big kids — Andrew and Callie and Keith. You have worksheets. They are about letters and sounds. My assistant, Miss Hannie, will help you with them. I will be working with Emily and Sari."

Keith raised his hand then. "Excuse me, but what do we call you?" he asked.

"While we are in school, you call me Miss Karen," I told him.

"Even me?" Andrew wanted to know.

"Even you. And remember to raise your hand."

My students got to work. I sat on the floor with Emily and Sari.

"Time to learn the alphabet," I told them.

Emily and Sari were a lot more interested in some My Little Pony dolls. I had to hide them. (Emily cried.)

We stuck to my schedule all morning. My students finished worksheets. They practiced writing their letters. (Emily and Sari just practiced tracing.) I read them a story. We discussed the story. They had a ten-minute rest. Oh, and they had snacktime. Just before the morning ended, I gave my students homework. I would help Emily with hers, Hannie would help Sari with hers, and the big kids were on their own.

"See you tomorrow!" I called when Miss Karen's School was over. "Remember to bring your homework with you."

10

"We Want Recess!"

"Andrew," I said on Saturday night, "have you done your homework yet?" (Andrew was just sitting on the couch, watching TV.)

"No," he said.

"But Andrew, you have to do it. You have to bring it with you to school tomorrow. And it has to be finished. That is the point of homework."

"Okay. I will do it when this show is over."

While Andrew watched his show, I made

Emily work on tracing again. That was her homework. Then I handed Andrew another worksheet.

"Do I *have* to do this?" wailed Andrew.

"Yes," I replied. "This is real school, remember?"

I hoped Keith and Callie and Sari were doing their homework.

On Sunday morning I marched into the playroom right after breakfast. I wanted to make sure Miss Karen's School was ready for its students and for another day of work.

School was supposed to start at ten o'clock. But at five minutes to ten o'clock, I was the only one in the playroom.

"Andrew!" I called. "Emily! Hurry up. You will be late for school!"

I practically had to carry them into the playroom. Just as they were sitting down, Hannie and Sari arrived.

"Oh, good. You are right on time," I said. "But where are Callie and Keith? And Andrew, where is your homework paper?"

Andrew went looking for his worksheet, while I went looking for Callie and Keith. I found them playing at their house. They had forgotten about Miss Karen's School. And they had not done their homework.

Boo and bullfrogs.

School started half an hour late that morning.

"You will all have to stay an extra half hour to make up for it," I said. "School will not end until twelve-thirty today."

"No fair!" cried Andrew.

"No calling out," I reminded him. "Now it is time for writing practice. Hannie, you help Emily and Sari with their tracing. Today I will work with the big kids." I pulled out the sheets with the letters of the alphabet on them. "Okay. Practice your letters again," I said.

"Miss Karen? Could we practice words?" asked Callie.

"Yeah, we want to write words," added Keith.

"Not yet. You are not ready."

Everyone worked quietly for five minutes. Then I looked over at Emily and Sari. I saw that they were not working at all. They were playing with My Little Pony dolls.

Before I could say anything, Andrew announced, "We want recess!"

"But it is not recess time yet," I told him.

"Maybe it is time for art," said Callie hopefully.

"Pony!" cried Sari happily.

I could see that my students did not care much about learning. Well, I would change that. I cleared my throat. "Ahem!"

"Uh-oh," said Andrew.

"Everybody! Attention, please! No wiggling, no talking, no My Little Ponies! This is worktime."

My students went back to work.

At twelve-thirty, I said, "Okay, school is over."

"Yea!" cried Andrew.

I frowned at him. Then I said, "Before

you leave, let me give you your homework. It is due two weeks from yesterday, when you come back to Miss Karen's School."

"Nuts," said Andrew.

Chocolate Factory Day

Ms. Colman let Mr. Howard be our teacher more and more. He was in charge of our class longer and longer each day. Sometimes Ms. Colman sat in the back of our room and watched Mr. Howard. Sometimes she sat in the back of our room and worked on lesson plans or looked in our workbooks. And sometimes she left the room.

Mr. Howard had finished reading *Charlie and the Chocolate Factory* to us. That was fine with me. Now we were doing other things.

In math we were measuring things. We measured out a little chocolate factory and built it with blocks. In art we colored portraits of Charlie Bucket and the other people in the book. In writing we were working on our own ending to the story. We pretended the book needed another chapter. I liked our chocolate factory unit. But I did not like Mr. Howard.

One day Mr. Howard said, "Class, I have an announcement." (I wondered if it would be as good as Ms. Colman's Surprising Announcements.) "You have been working hard and I am proud of you. I have been working hard, too. I will only be your teacher for about two and a half more weeks. I thought we could do something special on our last day together. So I have decided that we will hold Chocolate Factory Day. Chocolate Factory Day will be a program for your families and friends. You may invite your parents and grandparents and younger brothers and sisters and a few friends to come to our class in the afternoon. We will perform songs and skits about *Charlie and the Chocolate Factory*. And we will serve chocolate candy that we're going to make ourselves."

I glanced at Ricky Torres. I was surprised. Mr. Howard's announcement was pretty good after all. In fact, it was great.

I raised my hand and wiggled my fingers around. I waited for Mr. Howard to call on me. Then I said, "Oh, Mr. Howard, I just love being onstage. I love singing and dancing and acting. I might be an actress one day. This program is going to be terrific!"

Mr. Howard smiled at me. "Thank you, Karen," he said.

I really might be an actress one day. Nancy too. I like having an audience. Some people do not, but I do.

I tried to imagine myself on Chocolate Factory Day. I would stand in the front of the class before all the parents and other guests. Maybe I would sing a song I wrote myself. And I would be the star.

From next to me, I heard Ricky whisper,

"Pssst, Karen! Pay attention! Mr. Howard is talking to us."

I sat still. I listened to Mr. Howard.

". . . so we need to think about our program," he was saying.

I raised my hand again. When Mr. Howard called on me, I said, "I think we should put on four small skits, and then we should all sing a song together. Some people do not like to be in skits, you know. But they probably would not mind singing a — "

"Okay, Karen," said Mr. Howard. "That is a good idea."

I raised my hand again. Before Mr. Howard called on me, I said, "Can Hannie and Nancy and I put on a skit by ourselves? We could write one about different kinds of candy."

"We'll see," said Mr. Howard.

"Oh, and you know the chocolates you said we are going to make? Could we make chocolate-covered cherries? Nannie loves those. She — "

"Karen," said Mr. Howard. "Excuse me.

Would you let me talk for a minute? And would you please give your classmates a chance to say something? They would like to plan the program, too."

Well, for heaven's sake. I knew it. I just knew it. Mr. Howard did not like me. He did not want to hear my ideas. Ms. Colman always wanted to hear my ideas. But not Mr. Howard.

Smelly old Mr. Howard.

Smelly Mr. Howard

One Monday morning when I walked into my classroom, I had a surprise. Guess who was already sitting at Ms. Colman's desk. Mr. Howard. He was going to be our teacher for the next two weeks. Ms. Colman would not be our teacher at all. Bullfrogs.

I sat down at my desk. My desk is smack in front of the teacher's desk. In fact, they touch each other.

"Good morning, Karen," said Mr. Howard. He smiled at me.

"Good morning," I answered. Maybe

Mr. Howard liked me after all. I could not tell. But I decided I would try to be nice to him.

I moved to the back of the room. Hannie and Nancy were there. They were sitting on their desks and talking. Nancy was wearing a flowery dress with a wide lace collar. On her feet were her black tappy party shoes with bows. She had tied a ribbon in her hair.

When Nancy saw me, she sighed. Then she said dreamily, "Just think. Two whole weeks with Mr. Howard."

"And Chocolate Factory Day," I added.

"With real chocolate," said Hannie.

"With Mr. Howard," repeated Nancy.

Soon Mr. Howard began to take roll. As I sat down at my desk, I told myself again to be nice to Mr. Howard. And to be polite. And to be a help. I decided to help him be just like Ms. Colman.

During science, Mr. Howard asked Natalie to read aloud.

I raised my hand right away and called out, "Oh, Mr. Howard, Ms. Colman doesn't make Natalie read aloud unless she wants to. Because of her lisp."

"But *I* am asking her to," said Mr. Howard.

When art class was over, Mr. Howard collected the pictures we had colored of imaginary factories. He put them in our folders.

"Oh, Mr. Howard!" I called out. "Ms. Colman always puts our pictures on the bulletin board. So we can be proud of them."

"The bulletin board is full, Karen," said Mr. Howard.

I turned around to look at Ms. Colman. She was sitting in the back of the room. She was watching Mr. Howard. But Ms. Colman did not look back at me. She began to write in a notebook. Anyway, she had not said a word all day. She was letting Mr. Howard be in charge.

I decided that maybe Mr. Howard did not want my help.

On Tuesday, I did not help Mr. Howard, but I was still trying to be nice and polite. I thought he would want to know that he had a stain on his necktie. It looked like tomato soup.

"Mr. Howard?" I said. (I forgot to raise my hand.) "You have a stain on your necktie. You should probably wash it out."

Mr. Howard's face turned red. But all he said was, "Karen, can't you remember to raise your hand?"

Then *my* face turned red.

On Wednesday, I was a little noisy. (I got excited thinking about Chocolate Factory Day.) When I am noisy around Ms. Colman, she just says to me, "Indoor voice, Karen."

But Mr. Howard must not know about indoor voices. *He* said, "Karen Brewer, stop your shouting! I cannot hear myself think."

Humphh.

On Thursday, I had a lot of ideas about

Chocolate Factory Day. I kept calling them out. Do you know what Mr. Howard finally said to me? He said, "Karen, you are too noisy. Please keep quiet for the rest of the afternoon."

Smelly old Mr. Howard.

Karen on Strike

I decided I hated Mr. Howard. He was not just smelly. He was mean. I knew he did not like me.

So I hated him.

I wished the next week were over and he would go away.

I wished I did not have to go to school until he had gone away.

But I knew I had to go to school. I could not pretend to be sick for a whole week. Still — I did not have to talk to Mr. Howard, did I? After all, he had told me to keep quiet for the rest of the afternoon. Well, I would do better than that. I would keep quiet for the next week.

I went on strike.

At home on Friday morning, even before breakfast, I got out a piece of notebook paper. Then I found a red marker. In huge letters I wrote *ON STRICK* on the paper. That did not look quite right, so I found another piece of paper and wrote *ON STRIKE*. There. That was better. I folded the paper and tucked it into my backpack. I tossed in a roll of tape, too.

"Karen, what are you doing?" asked Andrew. He was peering into my room.

"I am going on strike," I told him. Then I had to explain to him what that meant.

"I hope your strike works," said Andrew.

"Thank you," I replied.

When I reached my classroom, I taped the sign to my shirt. Then I folded my arms and sat at my desk.

"Hi, Karen!" said Hannie when she ran into the room.

I did not answer her, since I was on strike. But I did not want her to think I was mad at her, so I pointed to my sign.

"You're on strike?" said Hannie, and I nodded.

"Hi, Karen!" called Ricky when he entered the room.

I pointed to my sign again.

By the time Mr. Howard showed up, half the class knew I was on strike. (Ms. Colman was not in the room. She was not going to come until the afternoon. She had said so the day before.)

Soon Mr. Howard called the roll. "Karen Brewer," he said.

I did not answer.

"Karen?" he said again. He was looking right at me.

Hannie raised her hand. "Mr. Howard," she said, "Karen is on strike."

Mr. Howard peered at my sign. His face grew red, but he did not say anything. He continued taking the roll.

Guess what I did all morning at school.

Nothing. I just sat at my desk. I did not talk, I did not work. At lunchtime I followed my class to the cafeteria, but that was only so I would not get stuck sitting alone in the classroom with Mr. Howard.

After lunch came recess. And after recess, my classmates and I returned to our room. Ms. Colman was there. She was talking to Mr. Howard. When she saw me, she said, "Karen, I would like to speak with you, please."

Ms. Colman and I sat together at the back of the room. My teacher looked at my sign. She said, "I understand you are on strike."

I nodded. "Yes. And I am going to stay on strike all next week. I am going to stay on strike until Mr. Howard has left. I am even going to stay on strike during Chocolate Factory Day." (I hoped I would ruin Chocolate Factory Day for Mr. Howard.)

Ms. Colman did not look happy. "I am afraid you may not do that, Karen. If you do, you will need to talk to the principal. And I will have to call your parents. School is a place for working, not striking. I would like you to try to get along with Mr. Howard."

My mouth dropped open. Go to the principal's office? Ms. Colman had never, ever said anything like that to me. So I told her that my strike was over. But I was not sure I meant it.

The Flunk-Outs

Another big-house weekend had arrived. It was time for two more days of Miss Karen's School. I wondered whether my students would remember to come. I wondered whether they would bring their homework.

By 10:05 every one of my students had arrived.

Not one of them had brought his homework.

"In real school you have to bring in your homework!" I cried. (I was still mad at Mr.

Howard, and my mad feelings were spilling over.) Andrew raised his hand. "I will remember to do my homework *tonight*."

"I hope so," I told him. (Andrew stuck out his lower lip, but I did not pay any attention to that.) "Okay. Reading time," I announced. "The big kids will work with me on flash cards. Emily and Sari will work with Miss Hannie on their letters." I paused. Then I added, "*Not* on My Little Ponies. Reading is fifteen minutes long."

After reading came art. "Today," I said, "we are going to color pages from my coloring book. Please use the colors I tell you to use."

"Excuse me, Miss Karen," said Hannie. "Why do they have to use the colors you say to use? Why can't they choose their own colors?"

"Hannie," I whispered loudly. "Leave things to me. I am the teacher. And you are just my helper."

Hannie did not answer. But I think she stuck her tongue out at me. I turned around fast, trying to see. But she was already handing out crayons to my students.

"Now, everybody," I said, "make the tops of the trees green and the trunks brown. Make the grass green, too."

"I want to make the top of my tree red," said Callie. "The tree outside my window is turning red."

And Hannie said to me, "Karen, Emily and Sari are not coloring. They *can't*. They are just scribbling. Emily is scribbling with Dusty Rose, and Sari is scribbling with Burnt Sienna."

I sighed. I did not know what to do. Finally I let the scribblers scribble, but I told Callie she had to color her tree green.

When art was over, I read a book to my students. It was called *Outside Over There*.

After that it was time for writing. I handed out tracing worksheets. The big kids were going to trace the alphabet again. Sari and Emily were going to trace shapes.

Andrew pouted when he saw his worksheet. "Letters *again*?" he said.

"Yup," I replied. "Letters make words. And you are the one who wanted to learn to write words," I reminded him.

"I know," said Andrew. "But I do not want to trace anymore."

"Then how are you going to learn to write?"

"I don't know. But no more tracing."

"No tracing for Callie and me, either," said Keith. He crossed his arms.

I crossed my arms, too. "All right," I said. "Then I am flunking you. All of you." I glanced at Sari and Emily. "Sari and Emily, too," I added. "Because they are not tracing. Everybody gets an F today."

"You mean we are flunk-outs?" cried Andrew.

I nodded my head firmly. "Yes."

"But I am only four!" said Andrew.

"Sorry," I replied. "Okay. I guess school is over for today. Your homework is to practice writing your names. See you to-morrow."

"Maybe," said Keith and Callie.

Andrew on Strike

I do not know if Andrew did his home-work on Saturday night. I did not pester him about it. I had decided that if he was going to be in real school, then he should remember to do his homework himself.

On Sunday morning I walked Emily into Miss Karen's School. I sat her in her place on the floor.

"Now we just have to wait for the other students," I told her.

At ten o'clock sharp, Hannie came over. She brought Sari with her. Hannie and Sari and Emily and I waited for five minutes.

At 10:05, I said, "Andrew and Callie and Keith are late. I will go find Andrew." I paused. Then I added, "I hope he did his homework."

I was just about to step into the hall when I heard footsteps. Then my other students entered the room. They walked silently to their table.

"Good morning," I said as they sat down.

At first they did not answer. Finally Andrew said, "We are on strike."

"On strike?" I repeated.

"On strike?" said Hannie. "You mean like when Karen was on strike in Mr. Howard's class on Friday?"

Andrew did not say anything. Neither did Keith and Callie. They just sat at their table with their hands folded.

I decided to pretend they were not on strike.

"Okay," I said. "I will now take attendance. When I call your name, raise your hand and say, 'Here.' " (To be on the safe side, I started with the little kids.) "Emily?" I said.

Hannie nudged Emily. She helped her raise her hand. "Here!" said Emily.

I called Sari's name. Hannie nudged Sari. "Here!" said Sari.

I called Andrew's name. No answer.

"Callie?" (No answer.) "Keith?" (No answer.) "Does that mean you are absent?" I asked. I thought Andrew might laugh at my joke, but he did not. Neither did Callie or Keith. I glanced at Hannie. She shrugged.

"Well," I went on, "today we will have writing first. Who remembered to do their homework?"

After a pause, Hannie said, "I do not think you gave any homework to Sari and Emily. So they did not do any."

"Right," I agreed. "Andrew and Callie and Keith, did you practice writing your names? . . . Come on, did you?"

74

Still they would not answer me. They would not even look at me.

"All right. I will work with Sari and Emily," I said. I sat on the floor with them. Hannie sat next to me. "Are you ready to try tracing some fun letters?" I asked.

Sari and Emily had found three old Barbie dolls. Sari was patting their hair. Emily was putting one in a baby doll's bed.

"No dolls now," I told my students. "Time to work." I took Emily's doll out of the bed. I moved it away from her.

"Mine!" shrieked Emily.

"Not now. Okay. If you do not want to trace, you can practice learning your letters. Emily, Sari, what is this letter?"

"Play doll?" asked Sari.

I sighed. Then I stood up and looked around the classroom. Three of my students were sitting, doing nothing. One of them was playing with a Barbie doll. One was crying. (Emily.) It was not much of a school.

"All right," I said. "School is closed."

"Good," said Andrew. He and Keith and Callie ran out of the room. Hannie led Emily and Sari out. And I hung a *Closed* sign on the door.

Karen Is Mean

I decided my school was a flunk-out. My school, my very own school.

After Hannie and my students left, I stood in the hallway. I looked at the *Closed* sign hanging on the doorknob. The sign made me very sad, so I walked away from it.

I sat in my room for a while. I read a chapter in a book. I drew a picture with my markers. Then I looked at my watch. It was still only eleven-thirty in the morning. The weekend was not over. All of Sunday afternoon was left, plus a teeny bit of the morning. Maybe I could find someone to play with me. I wandered downstairs. I wandered onto the front porch. Hannie was probably at her house. She would play with me.

Just as I was about to run across the street, Hannie's front door opened. Out came Hannie . . . and Nancy. What was Nancy doing at the Papadakises' house? Why hadn't she and Hannie called me? The Three Musketeers always play together. Oh, well. Maybe they were on their way over to the big house. I waited for a moment. No. My two best friends sat down together under a tree.

"Hey! Hey, you guys!" I shouted.

Hannie looked up. "Hi," she said.

"Come on over here!" I called.

Hannie and Nancy glanced at each other. Finally Hannie said, "No thanks. That's okay."

"Well then, I will come over there," I said. I dashed across the street. "Why didn't you want to come to my house?" I asked my friends.

Hannie and Nancy looked at each other again. Then Nancy said, "Karen, I do not really want to play with you today."

"Why not?"

"Because I am mad at you."

"Mad at me? What did I do?"

"You were not very nice to Mr. Howard on Friday. I did not like your strike. You hurt Mr. Howard's feelings," said Nancy.

"But *he* is not nice to *me!*" I cried.

Nancy shrugged. "Everyone else likes him."

"So?"

"So are you going to be on strike next week, too?"

"I don't know. I have not made up my mind yet," I said.

"Because if you are on strike, you will ruin Chocolate Factory Day."

"I know," I replied. I grinned.

"Well, excuse me, Karen, but *I* am looking forward to Chocolate Factory Day," said Nancy. "I do not want you to ruin it. If you ruin it, you ruin it for me and everyone else. You are being mean. And you are being especially mean to Mr. Howard."

"Why are you taking *his* side?" I yelled. "I thought you were one of my best friends. Best friends are supposed to take the *same* side."

"How can I take your side when you are being stupid?" asked Nancy.

"Stupid? I am not being stupid!"

"Are too."

"Am not."

I looked at Hannie. She shrugged. "This is your fight," she said to Nancy and me. "I am striking the fight." She closed her mouth.

I turned back to Nancy. I narrowed my eyes. "Mr. Howard is not nice. He is not fair. And his hair smells."

"Karen," said Nancy, "why don't you just go home?"

So I did.

A Good Teacher

I ran across the street. I ran across our lawn. I ran through the front door of the big house and all the way up the stairs to my room. Then I flopped on my bed.

I held Tickly in one hand and I hugged Moosie with the other. I cried a little bit. When I finished crying, I grumbled to Moosie. "Nancy is horrible. She is a meanie-mo. She is my best enemy, not my best friend. We should kick her out of the Three Musketeers. Mr. Howard is horrible, too. I do not care what Ms. Colman said. I am going to be on strike again tomorrow. And Andrew — "

"Karen?"

I glanced up. Kristy was standing in the doorway. "Hi," I said.

"Is something wrong?" Kristy wanted to know.

"Is *some*thing wrong?" I repeated. "*Every*thing is wrong."

Kristy sat next to me on the bed. "Do you want to tell me about it?" she asked. She picked up one of my dolls and began to braid its hair. "Well," I said slowly. "It's school. Real school and Miss Karen's School. They are both a big mess."

"What is the matter with Miss Karen's School?" asked Kristy.

"Nobody will listen to me. Nobody will do what I say. I am in charge!" I cried. "My students do not do their homework — "

"You assigned homework?" said Kristy.

I nodded. "The first time I *made* Andrew do his. But he does not remember on his own. Neither do Callie and Keith. And they

will not color their pictures the way I say to, or practice tracing their letters. Plus, I made a schedule, but the kids will *not* do their tracing during tracing time. The big kids want to do other things, and the little kids keep playing with dolls and stuff." I paused. "So yesterday I flunked everyone for the day. And today, Andrew and Callie and Keith were on strike. They just sat at their table. They would not even talk. Finally I closed Miss Karen's School."

Kristy raised her eyebrows. "I saw the sign on the door," she said.

I sighed. "I must not be a very good teacher."

"Well," said Kristy, "I will tell you something. One of my best teachers ever was Mrs. Kushel. She taught me a long time ago, but I will always remember her, because she made learning fun. And she listened to her students. She made us feel important. You know what? I think school is not just about reading and writing. It is also about helping kids to feel good about themselves. Did you try that, Karen?"

"Not really," I admitted. "I guess I was bossy instead. I ordered the kids around, and I made up that schedule, and I hardly ever listened to my students. I did not give them a chance."

"Karen," said Kristy, "you said you were having problems in real school, too. Are those problems with your student teacher?"

"With Mr. Howard? Yes," I said.

"Did you give Mr. Howard a chance?"

"No. I did not like him the very first time I met him. He uses smelly stuff in his hair. I know that is not a good reason to dislike him. But Kristy," I rushed on, when I saw the look on her face, "Mr. Howard did not give *me* a chance. He decided I talk too much. And that was that. *He* was not fair to *me*. You know I do not have trouble in school. I just have trouble with Mr. Howard."

"Maybe you should talk to him," said Kristy.

"Maybe," I replied. I had a lot to think about.

Gold Stars

When Kristy left my room, I stayed right where I was. I was still holding Tickly and Moosie. I thought about Mr. Howard. I thought about the look on his face when he saw my *ON STRIKE* sign. I remembered how I felt when Andrew and Keith and Callie went on strike. I thought about flunking my students. I remembered Andrew saying, "You mean we are flunk-outs? But I am only four!" I thought about how bad I had made him feel.

Then I sat up straight. I dropped Moosie

and Tickly. I had just had a wonderful idea. I could still fix things. I looked at my clock. Yes, I had enough time.

I ran outside. "Andrew!" I called. "Andrew, where are you?"

I found Andrew in the backyard. He was playing with Callie and Keith. "What do you want?" he asked. "School is over."

"I want to say I am sorry," I said. "I am sorry I was such a bad teacher. I ordered you around and I did not listen to you."

"And you were bossy," said Keith.

"And I was bossy," I agreed. "But now I want to start over. If you will come back to school, everything will be different. I promise. I will listen to you, and we will not stick to my schedule every second, and you can use any color crayons you want."

"Do we still have to call you Miss Karen?" asked Andrew.

"Only if you want to," I told him. Then I added, "Oh, and I am going to make school fun from now on. So will you come back to the classroom with me?"

Andrew and Callie and Keith looked at each other. Finally Andrew said, "I guess so. But if you are mean, Karen, we will go on strike again."

"Okay," I said. "That is fair."

I led my students into the house and upstairs to the playroom. I did not bother to look for Emily. And I did not call Hannie or Sari, because I knew Hannie was still playing with Nancy. My students sat at their table. They looked at me. They waited for me to say something.

"Today," I began, "we are going to read a story first. We will read — " I paused. "Well, what would *you* like to read?"

"*Mike Mulligan and His Steam Shovel!*" cried Callie.

"Yes!" agreed Andrew and Keith.

So that is the story I read. When I finished, I handed out paper and crayons. "Now you may draw pictures of Mike or anybody else in the story," I said. I helped my students write sentences about their pictures. I wrote some of the words and

88

they wrote some of the words. I had to tell them what letters to make, though.

Even so, Andrew suddenly jumped up out of his chair. "Hey!" he cried. "I am writing! I am really writing!"

Callie and Keith looked down at their papers. "Hey, yeah!" exclaimed Keith. "We are writing, too!"

Pretty soon my students were tired of coloring. So I handed out worksheets. This time I let them fill in the worksheets together. I decided it was okay for them to talk to each other.

At last school was over. I collected everybody's work. I pulled out their best papers and stuck gold stars on them.

"Gold stars!" cried Andrew. "We really are not flunk-outs anymore."

"Are you *sure* school is over?" asked Callie. "Can't we stay a *little* longer?"

"I'm sorry," I said. "Andrew and I have to leave. But we will see you in two weeks. And your homework is . . . no homework!"

90

Friends Again

When Seth drove me to school on Monday morning, I did not bring my strike sign with me. I left it lying on my bed. I had been thinking about my talk with Kristy, and about not giving Mr. Howard a chance. I had decided to give him *one more chance*. But if he still did not listen to me, and if he still told me to keep quiet, then I would go on strike again. (I would not go on strike just for smelly hair, though.)

When I walked into my classroom, Mr. Howard was already sitting at his desk.

"Good morning, Karen," he said. "I was hoping you would come in early. I would like to talk to you."

Uh-oh, I thought. This sounds like trouble.

"Please sit down," said Mr. Howard, after I had put my things in my cubby.

I sat at my desk. I was looking straight at Mr. Howard. I folded my hands and waited for him to say something.

Mr. Howard cleared his throat. "I am glad to see that your strike is over," he began. "It *is* over, isn't it?"

"For now," I answered.

"Would you like to tell me why you went on strike?"

"Because you were not fair to me. You did not listen to me. You told me to be quiet for a whole afternoon! Ms. Colman has never told me anything like that. And she always listens."

"That may be. But, Karen, from the moment I came to your classroom, I felt that you were not pleased with me."

"I know. I did not give you a chance. But you did not give *me* a chance, Mr. Howard. I never have trouble in school or with Ms. Colman. Well, hardly ever," I said.

"How about a deal?" asked Mr. Howard. "Will you make a deal with me? I will listen to your ideas *if* you promise not to strike again. And if you will join in on Chocolate Factory Day. And remember to raise your hand, wait to be called on, and use your indoor voice."

"Deal," I said. Then I grinned at Mr. Howard.

A few minutes later Nancy came into the room. I followed her to her desk. "Nancy," I said, "I need to talk to you. I want to tell you I am sorry. And I am not going to strike Chocolate Factory Day. Mr. Howard and I made a deal."

"You did?" said Nancy.

I nodded. "Yup. I really am sorry, Nancy. I am sorry I was mean. I am sorry I was unfair. I want to be your friend again."

"Good," replied Nancy. "I was hoping you would say that."

"Hey! Are you guys talking again?" Hannie had come into the room. She ran to us.

"Yes," said Nancy and I at the same time. And I added, "I told Nancy I was sorry I was so mean. Hannie, I was mean to you too. I ordered you around when we were teaching. And I said you could only be my helper. That was not fair. You can be a real teacher if you want. And we will change the name of our school. It does not have to be Miss Karen's School."

"I thought the school was closed," said Hannie.

I shook my head. "Nope. It opened again." I told her what had happened after I talked to Kristy. "So our students will be back in two weeks," I went on. "Hey, Nancy," I said, "are you *sure* you do not want to be a teacher too?"

But Nancy was gazing at Mr. Howard again. She was still in love with him. Oh, well. At least our fight was over.

Mrs. Howard

My last week with Mr. Howard was not too bad. I had to work *extra* hard to remember to raise my hand and not yell out. But at least Mr. Howard called on me. He did not have to tell me to keep quiet anymore. And even though I wanted to tell Mr. Howard about all the things he was doing wrong, and about the lettuce that got stuck on his front tooth, and especially about his smelly hair tonic, I did not. I knew that on Monday Mr. Howard would be gone, and Ms. Colman would be back. My problems would be over. So I did not have to go on strike again, and Mr. Howard was nice to me.

Friday was Mr. Howard's last day in our classroom. It was also Chocolate Factory Day. My friends and I were excited. We had planned skits and practiced songs. We had made chocolate candies. And we had invited our families to come to our room after recess on Friday afternoon. Here is who was coming from my two families: Mommy, Andrew, and Daddy.

On Friday, our guests began to arrive. My classmates and I had moved our desks against the walls. We had lined up our chairs at the back of the room. They were for our guests. We stood in the front of the room and waited. When the people in our families came in, we waved to them.

"Nancy, there are your parents!" I whispered. "Hannie, there are your mom and Sari!"

"Karen!" Hannie hissed back. "Here comes your dad!"

We watched Ricky's parents arrive. Bobby's mother came with Bobby's little sister. The twins' father came.

"Who's that?" Nancy whispered to me a little later.

I looked at the woman who had entered the room. "Is she Pamela's mother?" I suggested.

Nancy shook her head. "I don't think so."

The woman sat in the front row of chairs. We would have to wait to find out who she was.

When all of our guests had found seats, Mr. Howard stepped to the front of the room. "Welcome," he said. "Welcome, parents and grandparents and brothers and sisters and friends. Thank you for coming. We have been working very hard to put together this program for you. Get ready to enter the world of Charlie Bucket. We hope you will enjoy Chocolate Factory Day.

"Before the program begins I would like to thank Ms. Colman for her help." Mr.

Howard smiled at Ms. Colman who was sitting in the back of the room with the guests. "And," he went on, "I would like to thank my wife for coming." (The woman in the front row gave Mr. Howard a little wave.) "Okay, boys and girls," Mr. Howard said to us. "You may begin."

I hardly heard what Mr. Howard had just said. I turned to Nancy. Mr. Howard had a *wife*? That woman was *Mrs.* Howard? That meant Nancy could not be in love with Mr. Howard anymore.

Nancy had turned pale. She was staring at Mrs. Howard. I nudged her. "We have to sing our song," I whispered.

So our program began. My classmates and I sang our songs and put on our skits. Then we passed around the candies we had made. Our guests talked and laughed. They ate the candy.

Nancy just stared at Mrs. Howard.

At last it was time to say good-bye to our student teacher.

"You know what?" said Nancy after we

had shouted good-bye and thank you. "I thought it would be so, so hard to say good-bye to Mr. Howard. But it was not hard at all. I will miss him a little. But I am not in love with him anymore."

"And Ms. Colman will be our teacher again," I added.

"Karen?" said Nancy. "Hannie? Do you think I could help you with your school after all?"

"Sure," said Hannie.

"We need another teacher," I added.

The Three Musketeers put their arms around each other. "Best friends forever!" we cried.

About the Author

ANN M. MARTIN lives in New York City and loves animals, especially cats. She has two cats of her own, Mouse and Rosie.

Other books by Ann M. Martin that you might enjoy are *Stage Fright*; *Me and Katie (the Pest)*; and the books in *The Baby-sitters Club* series.

Ann likes ice cream and *I Love Lucy*. And she has her own little sister, whose name is Jane.

Little Sister

Don't miss #42

KAREN'S PIZZA PARTY

"You will get the pizza soon," I said to
Bobby. "I promise."

"But you promised before."

"This time I *really* promise."

As soon as I was off the phone, I went
looking for Mommy. "Do you think I can
get free Pizza Express pizza for my
friends?" I asked her. "Since I am the Pizza
Queen."

Mommy shook her head. "Sorry, honey.
I don't think so. Mr. Rush did not mention
it. Besides, he is paying you a lot of money.
And no," Mommy went on, "you may not
ask Mr. Rush about it."

I couldn't? Uh-oh.

LITTLE  APPLE®

BABY SITTERS

Little Sister™

by Ann M. Martin,
author of The Baby-sitters Club ®

☐	MQ44300-3	#1	Karen's Witch	$2.95
☐	MQ44259-7	#2	Karen's Roller Skates	$2.95
☐	MQ44299-7	#3	Karen's Worst Day	$2.95
☐	MQ44264-3	#4	Karen's Kittycat Club	$2.95
☐	MQ44258-9	#5	Karen's School Picture	$2.95
☐	MQ44298-8	#6	Karen's Little Sister	$2.95
☐	MQ44257-0	#7	Karen's Birthday	$2.95
☐	MQ42670-2	#8	Karen's Haircut	$2.95
☐	MQ43652-X	#9	Karen's Sleepover	$2.95
☐	MQ43651-1	#10	Karen's Grandmothers	$2.95
☐	MQ43650-3	#11	Karen's Prize	$2.95
☐	MQ43649-X	#12	Karen's Ghost	$2.95
☐	MQ43648-1	#13	Karen's Surprise	$2.95
☐	MQ43646-5	#14	Karen's New Year	$2.95
☐	MQ43645-7	#15	Karen's in Love	$2.95
☐	MQ43644-9	#16	Karen's Goldfish	$2.95
☐	MQ43643-0	#17	Karen's Brothers	$2.95
☐	MQ43642-2	#18	Karen's Home-Run	$2.75
☐	MQ43641-4	#19	Karen's Good-Bye	$2.95
☐	MQ44823-4	#20	Karen's Carnival	$2.95
☐	MQ44824-2	#21	Karen's New Teacher	$2.95
☐	MQ44833-1	#22	Karen's Little Witch	$2.95
☐	MQ44832-3	#23	Karen's Doll	$2.95
☐	MQ44859-5	#24	Karen's School Trip	$2.95
☐	MQ44831-5	#25	Karen's Pen Pal	$2.95
☐	MQ44830-7	#26	Karen's Ducklings	$2.95
☐	MQ44829-3	#27	Karen's Big Joke	$2.95
☐	MQ44828-5	#28	Karen's Tea Party	$2.95
☐	MQ44825-0	#29	Karen's Cartwheel	$2.75
☐	MQ45645-8	#30	Karen's Kittens	$2.95
☐	MQ45646-6	#31	Karen's Bully	$2.95
☐	MQ45647-4	#32	Karen's Pumpkin Patch	$2.95
☐	MQ45648-2	#33	Karen's Secret	$2.95
☐	MQ45650-4	#34	Karen's Snow Day	$2.95
☐	MQ45652-0	#35	Karen's Doll Hospital	$2.95
☐	MQ45651-2	#36	Karen's New Friend	$2.95
☐	MQ45653-9	#37	Karen's Tuba	$2.95
☐	MQ45655-5	#38	Karen's Big Lie	$2.95
☐	MQ45654-7	#39	Karen's Wedding	$2.95
☐	MQ47040-X	#40	Karen's Newspaper	$2.95
☐	MQ47041-8	#41	Karen's School	$2.95
☐	MQ47042-6	#42	Karen's Pizza Party	$2.95
☐	MQ46912-6	#43	Karen's Toothache	$2.95

More Titles... ➡

☐ MQ47043-4	#44	Karen's Big Weekend	$2.95
☐ MQ47044-2	#45	Karen's Twin	$2.95
☐ MQ47045-0	#46	Karen's Baby-sitter	$2.95
☐ MQ46913-4	#47	Karen's Kite	$2.95
☐ MQ47046-9	#48	Karen's Two Families	$2.95
☐ MQ47047-7	#49	Karen's Stepmother	$2.95
☐ MQ47048-5	#50	Karen's Lucky Penny	$2.95
☐ MQ48229-7	#51	Karen's Big Top	$2.95
☐ MQ48299-8	#52	Karen's Mermaid	$2.95
☐ MQ48300-5	#53	Karen's School Bus	$2.95
☐ MQ48301-3	#54	Karen's Candy	$2.95
☐ MQ48230-0	#55	Karen's Magician	$2.95
☐ MQ48302-1	#56	Karen's Ice Skates	$2.95
☐ MQ48303-X	#57	Karen's School Mystery	$2.95
☐ MQ48304-8	#58	Karen's Ski Trip	$2.95
☐ MQ48231-9	#59	Karen's Leprechaun	$2.95
☐ MQ48305-6	#60	Karen's Pony	$2.95
☐ MQ48306-4	#61	Karen's Tattletale	$2.95
☐ MQ48307-2	#62	Karen's New Bike	$2.95
☐ MQ25996-2	#63	Karen's Movie	$2.95
☐ MQ25997-0	#64	Karen's Lemonade Stand	$2.95
☐ MQ25998-9	#65	Karen's Toys	$2.95
☐ MQ26279-3	#66	Karen's Monsters	$2.95
☐ MQ26024-3	#67	Karen's Turkey Day	$2.95
☐ MQ26025-1	#68	Karen's Angel	$2.95
☐ MQ26193-2	#69	Karen's Big Sister	$2.95
☐ MQ26280-7	#70	Karen's Grandad	$2.95
☐ MQ26194-0	#71	Karen's Island Adventure	$2.95
☐ MQ26195-9	#72	Karen's New Puppy	$2.95
☐ MQ55407-7		BSLS Jump Rope Rhymes Pack	$5.99
☐ MQ47677-7		BSLS School Scrapbook	$2.95
☐ MQ43647-3		Karen's Wish Super Special #1	$3.25
☐ MQ44834-X		Karen's Plane Trip Super Special #2	$3.25
☐ MQ44827-7		Karen's Mystery Super Special #3	$3.25
☐ MQ45644-X		Karen, Hannie, and Nancy — The Three Musketeers Super Special #4	$2.95
☐ MQ45649-0		Karen's Baby Super Special #5	$3.50
☐ MQ46911-8		Karen's Campout Super Special #6	$3.25

Available wherever you buy books, or use this order form.